MW00901139

SNOOZE

by Brandi Russell

Special thanks to Randy for believing
in Snooze and in me! S.I.L.Y.
--B.R.

Dedicated to Kyler and Elle,
the nap-defying darlings who
inspired the creation of Snooze.
--B.R.

Howdy little lambchop!
My name is
Snooze E. Sheep.

According to my records, you aren't getting enough sleep.

Sleepy-Z Production

**Your Sleepy-Z production
is falling in the RED!
It's time to catch-up on those Zs,
you little sleepy head.**

I know a nap sounds
icky, yuck and blah --
like boring stew.

But you need your rest
to feel your best.

TO DO:

- ✓ EAT
- (SLEEP)
- ✓ PLAY
- ✓ BE HAPPY
- ✓ LAUGH
- ✓ ...AND POO

It's something you must do.

Let's play a game together that is super-duper fun.

Listen closely to the rules.
I'll start with number one...

"I'm a happy little napper!"

--is the phrase you need to say.

Then, crawl under your covers,

close your eyes and hit-the-hay.

You see, I am *napturnal*.
I am awake when
children sleep.
My magic energy
is fueled by
children's Sleepy-Zs.

While you are sleeping, I will hide you a surprise.

You never know what it will be or what will be the size.

When you wake-up from your nap,
look for Snooze Clues on the ground.

They will lead you to the place
where a surprise can be found.

I'm creative and I'm crafty,
so put on your thinking cap.
What Snooze surprise do you think you'll find
when you wake-up from your nap?

Caregiver Instructions:

You are the one who brings Snooze to life for your child. After reading the story together, guide your child to say the phrase, then *hit-the-hay*. While they are asleep, leave a trail of Snooze Clues leading them to a shenanigan or surprise to discover when they wake-up.

Print Snooze Clues, get ideas for surprises and shenanigans, and find additional sleep resources at:

www.snoozethesheep.com

Z Z Z
Z Z Z
Z Z Z

A few Snooze Clues just for you:

CPSIA information can be obtained at www.ICGtesting.com
Printed in the USA
BVIW12n1454200915
418789BV00004B/8